DEAD CHIMES

AMIE BORST

Summary: When eleven-year old Clarabelle Craven moves into a creepy house on Halloween night, she learns the Baba Yaga are stealing the souls of local children.

BISAC: JUVENILE FICTION/Horror. JUVENILE FICTION/Fairy Tales & Folklore/Country & Ethnic. JUVENILE FICTION/Paranormal, Occult & Supernatural.

For more information about this title, write us at Mystery Goose Press P.O. Box 86627 Vint Hill, VA 20187

Printed in the United States of America.
Paperback ISBN: 978-1-948882-31-6
Also available as an ebook

TICK TOCK

O n a gloomy autumn afternoon, roads slick with wet leaves, Clarabelle sat in the backseat of the family car as her father navigated around winding mountain roads. Trees stretched their leafless branches across the single lane path, but Clarabelle imagined they were boney fingers reaching for their next victim. In the distance, clouds swam past a rising crescent moon snugly nestled within the crevices of the mountains. Clarabelle swore they were shadows of long-ago lore dancing in the moonlight. Above, birds circled in the sky, their caws loud enough to drown out the hum of the engine. Clarabelle distinctly heard a teasing chant; "Go home Clarabelle Craven."

To which she silently replied, "Go away ravens!"

Her father suddenly swerved, jerking the car to the right, and sending them clear into a ditch. "Nearly killed us all!"

Mrs. Craven unfastened her seat belt and leapt out of the car. "It's just a baby."

"What is it?" Clarabelle swung her door open, fresh air biting at her cheeks.

"The death of me!" Mr. Craven said, throwing his hands into the air.

"Stop overreacting," Clarabelle's mother said, kneeling by the stunned animal. "It's only a bear cub."

Clarabelle inched closer. She knelt by her mother and inspected the creature. Long legs like a dog. A thick coat of fur in shades of brown and gray like a German Shepard. "I don't think that's a bear."

"Coyote," Mr. Craven said matter-of-factly, folding his arms. "They've been around these parts forever. Realtor told me they'll stay in the woods. Shouldn't bother us as long as we don't leave out food."

"Too bad she didn't mention they'd jump in front of your car." Mrs. Craven stood, hugged herself with a shiver, and climbed back into the passenger seat. "Getting chilly out there."

"Growing dark, too." Clarabelle's father put his hands on his hips and tipped his head back. He sucked in a big cleansing breath then blew it out as he rubbed his chest. "Nothing like that country air."

"Or pneumonia," Mrs. Craven said. "Get in the car. Don't want you to catch cold. And I don't want to unpack in the dark."

"Fine, fine," Mr. Craven said, half-annoyed. But he didn't budge. Just stood there admiring his surroundings. Cornfields to the left, a thick forest to the right, mountains straight ahead, and the skyscrapers of the city far behind us.

Mrs. Craven tapped her watch. "Tick tock. Time is running out."

"What are we going to do about the coyote? We can't just leave it there." Clarabelle nudged the creature with her boot. The coyote drew a breath, opened its eyes, and looked directly at the eleven-year-old girl whose straight brown hair nearly matched the shades of its own fur. Clarabelle let out an ear-piercing scream and the wild animal darted off into a forest of October leaves. "Did you see that?" she asked as her heart thudded in her chest. Scrambling into the car, Clarabelle was unsure if her breath was coming or going.

"You're just like your father," Mrs. Craven said. "Poor thing was scared."

"But it looked at me." Something very unsettling squirmed in Clarabelle's gut.

Mr. Craven climbed in the car. "At least it's not injured." He leaned over and pecked his wife on the cheek.

Clarabelle's stomach churned again. "I want to puke."

"Oh stop," Mrs. Craven said. She turned around and smiled at her daughter. "Now buckle up. You'll never know when another ditch will jump up at us."

"Very funny, Charlotte." Mr. Craven cranked the engine and it puttered to life. "This isn't like the city you know. I can blow my horn, run a red light, and speed around the block like nobody's business."

Mrs. Craven rolled her eyes. "Until you get caught. Fine's due next week, by the way. Better dig out your check book and get busy signing that note."

"Yeah, yeah." Mr. Craven pulled out onto

the single lane road without bothering to check over his shoulder. "Out here in the country, it's different. There's animals, nature. People take their time." A car horn blared behind them and Mr. Craven slammed on his breaks.

A black SUV sped past flashing its lights.

"Country folks will give you a run for your money." Mrs. Craven covered her mouth as she chuckled.

"Isn't that the realtor?" Mr. Craven leaned forward, squinting as he peered through the windshield. Dusk had rolled in, faster than it ever had in the bright lights of the big city. "What's she doing out here?"

Clarabelle was too busy watching the corn stalks in the field to worry about the realtor. The corn seemed to wave at her, beckoning her into their fields with a strange, and eerie rustling. Something else came through the corn, though. Clarabelle's eyes widened as she watched the creature barrel through the grass. It headed straight at them, unwilling to redirect its path as it charged at Clarabelle's door.

"Watch out!" Clarabelle screamed.

GOES THE CLOCK

Mr. Craven jerked the wheel. "Don't scream like that. You'll give us all a heart attack."

"It's coming," Clarabelle said, but by the time she'd uttered the words it was too late. The creature had lunged right at her door, shattering the glass of her window.

Mr. Craven's hands slipped on the steering wheel as the car veered off the road, straight into a ditch. It teetered on its side, just mere feet away from the edge of a cliff.

"What was that?" Mrs. Craven touched her forehead, a lump forming above her eyebrow.

"Your daughter overacting again. How

many times do we have to tell you not to carry on?"

Clarabelle wasn't listening though. She'd already opened her car door and slipped out. "It's dead," she said, studying the enormous creature that vaguely resembled a coyote.

"What are you doing out there?" Mrs. Craven unfastened her seat belt and scrambled out of the door. When she approached Clarabelle, she gasped. "Another one?"

Clarabelle nodded. She didn't need to say anything because the tremble in her hands said it all.

Mr. Craven cut the engine before hopping out of the vehicle. He bent down and examined the animal's abnormally large incisors. "Nothing we can do for it." He shook his head, inhaled the country air, and walked around to the other side of the car. "Give me a hand over here. Gotta get this thing out of the ditch before there isn't any daylight left." He turned and looked over his shoulder at the cliff. "Few more feet and we would have been toast."

"It was trying to kill us," Clarabelle said under her breath.

"It's just an animal," Mrs. Craven said. "It merely jumped at the wrong time."

Clarabelle shook her head. "Two of them? In a matter of minutes?"

"There's no time to worry about that now," Mr. Craven said as he waved his wife over. "Clarabelle, I'm going to need you to steer while your mom and I push. Just think of it like you're driving a go-kart."

"But I was like eight the last time I did that." Clarabelle surveyed the dashboard, looking closely at all the bells and whistles. She'd never been behind the wheel of a car before and it looked a bit intimidating.

"And you'll remember it like yesterday. It's like riding a bike. You don't forget how to do it." Mr. Craven was at her door now. He turned the key in the ignition and put the car in neutral. Before he returned to the passenger side, he patted his daughter on the shoulder. "Don't press anything, just cut the wheel to the left."

Clarabelle nodded, waited for the instruction, and turned. A moment later the car was out of the ditch, rolling downhill.

"Hit the brakes!" Mr. Craven shouted as he

ran alongside the car. He opened the door, pushing Clarabelle aside, and flung himself into the driver's seat. The car came to a screeching halt.

"Maybe this move wasn't such a great idea," Mrs. Craven said as she ran up to the car, panting.

"Nonsense." Mr. Craven wiped his brow, but he wasn't going to let his wife know he agreed with her. "Now, let's get this show back on the road."

"Good idea." Mrs. Craven, now serious, leaned forward. "You know, I think you're right."

Mr. Craven turned sharply. He couldn't believe his ears. "About what?"

"The realtor." Mrs. Craven fastened her seatbelt and leaned back. "Maybe we should hurry. I don't want to miss her."

Clarabelle sensed there might be more to this. Perhaps her mother was just as afraid of another coyote as she was.

Lead foot, Mr. Craven maneuvered down the one lane country road.

"I didn't mean you had to catch up to her right this instant." Mrs. Craven white knuckled the arm of her seat. "Take it easy. These roads aren't like the city."

"You're telling me," Clarabelle moaned from the backseat. She wasn't sure if it was motion sickness – being accustomed to city streets would do that to the best of people – or perhaps she was simply on imagination over-load. Nevertheless, Clarabelle felt the worst she'd ever felt in her entire life.

"Don't tell me how to drive, Charlotte. I can handle it." Despite Mr. Craven's best efforts, the car swayed around each turn, as if it would jeer off the path at any moment. It was almost as if the car had a mind of its own and wanted to slide down the hill whence it came.

Maybe, Clarabelle thought, *maybe that wasn't such a bad idea*. Then she'd be far away from this strange place and right back in the city with her friends. She was certain she could never love a place so filled with gloom.

"Tick tock goes the clock," Mrs. Craven said as the minutes ticked away along with the sunlight.

Hours later, the moon now high above the treetops in the darkest sky Clarabelle had ever seen, the Craven family arrived at their destination. A Queen Ann Victorian with a turret and front porch sat atop a grand hill, freckled with trees. Overgrown woods cradled the house on three sides.

The Craven family parked in the driveway and a chorus of howls swelled around them.

WHEN IT CHIMES

The hairs on Clarabelle's arms stood on end. She shivered and hugged herself in the moonlight.

"More coyotes," Mr. Craven said.

"Obviously." Clarabelle wasn't the least bit amused and upon seeing the home let out a sigh. "This decrepit old place is our house?" She inched her way out of the car, gritting her teeth. This was just another disappointment among the many. Not to mention they were miles from civilization. There'd probably be no one around to talk to, except her parents, of course.

Mrs. Craven, unaware of her daughter's

growing disdain, stretched, yawned then stepped out onto the lawn. "It's only for a year. After your father finishes his…" Mrs. Craven glanced at her husband still seated in the car and cleared her throat, whispering, "…his research."

Research. Like Clarabelle hadn't heard that one a million times before. What it really meant was that her father had lost his job. Again.

"Are you coming or not?" Clarabelle held the driver's door open and her father stepped out.

"Just a minute," Mr. Craven mumbled.

Mrs. Craven stood on the porch, ignoring the conversation between father and daughter. She held up a gift basket filled with fresh fruit and nuts. "The realtor was here! Look what she left for us."

"She's lucky those coyotes didn't take it." Mr. Craven scratched his chin. "She should have known better than to leave it out."

"Maybe she was in a hurry. Besides, we were late. If we'd been here like we were supposed to—"

Mr. Craven squinted an eye. "Enough, Charlotte."

While her parents argued over the reasons why they were late, which there were many, Clarabelle scanned the yard. In the thicket were glowing eyes, which Clarabelle was certain were more of those coyotes. Shivering, she hurried along the stone sidewalk (the crevices overflowed with weeds which seemed intent on tripping her). With each step she took, Clarabelle's legs became like lead. *I'm tired—that's all*, she thought, *my legs are heavy because of the long drive. Nothing quite like being trapped in a car all day.* When she glanced down, however, she saw half-dead weeds twisted in one giant mess around her ankles. She tore the nasty things off her legs and dusted her trousers with a very loud and very annoyed *a-hem*.

As she reached a finger out to press the buzzer, she couldn't help but notice the peeling paint on the front door. She picked at a piece, and with one flick of a finger, the paint came off in a sizeable chunk. "This place is falling apart," she called over her shoulder to her parents. "I bet it needs more than a paint job."

She guided her finger toward the doorbell again, but as she approached the spot there wasn't a doorbell after all, only a white moth. "That's funny…I thought…" Clarabelle shrugged, wrapped her fingers around the ugly raven-headed knocker in the middle of the door and struck it three times. As she did, she swore the knocker responded by saying, "Welcome home Clarabelle Craven."

But it was just her mother. "No need to knock, no one's in there. You'll need a key," Mrs. Craven called, only turning for a second to address her daughter (although never actually looking at her) and then quickly resumed the dialog with her husband.

From inside the house, the loud chimes of a clock began to sing.

"Do you hear that?" Clarabelle said. But her parents were too busy unloading items from the trunk to pay any mind to her. "When it chimes there's a ghastly little noise at the end."

Curious, and without a second of hesitation, Clarabelle picked up a skeleton key from under the entry mat and pushed it in the lock. She didn't know the key was there, she merely had a hunch. Perhaps the lump in the mat was her first clue. Still, it seemed odd that it should be so easy to gain entry. Before Clarabelle could turn the handle, the door creaked open.

IT SINGS A RHYME

Clarabelle peered inside, not stepping over the threshold. It was dark inside but not impossible to see. However, it was much too quiet for Clarabelle's liking. She preferred the sights and sounds of the big city she'd left behind. She stepped inside, inhaling the fragrance of lemon scented furniture polish. Despite the recent cleaning, nothing could ever mask the damp, musty odor that lingered within the walls of the house. *Why bother*, she thought, *it's old and dirty and disgusting*. Even the rotten floorboards and stains on the walls would be difficult to disguise with fresh paint.

As Mr. and Mrs. Craven carried on their

conversation in the driveway, Clarabelle stepped inside the house. In the foyer was a tall clock. Its pendulum swayed in rhythm to a steady beat. Tick tock, tock tick. Behind it, a staircase, which turned to the right, showcased dozens of clocks.

"Weird," Clarabelle said with a whisper. "I've never seen so many clocks in one place before."

A moment later Mr. Craven entered the house, carrying a large moving box (the only one he packed himself) which he placed at Clarabelle's feet. Mrs. Craven lugged in a suitcase and promptly dropped it at the door.

Mr. Craven tried a light switch, which only made a popping noise, and completely failed to produce a source of light. "Guess the landlord didn't bother to leave the electricity on." He walked to the kitchen, pulled a lighter from his pocket and attempted to light the stove. "Or the gas."

Then he went to the moving box he'd carried in, opened it and pulled out a flashlight. "Well now, that shines a little bit of light on the subject." Mr. Craven chuckled. He glanced around at the house, the light illuminating cobwebs in the rafters and a spider scurrying across the floor.

"No heat, no stove." Mrs. Craven placed her hands on her hips.

Clarabelle's stomach churned again. This time it was hunger—not motion sickness—and it produced a loud growl.

"What do you say we get a pizza for dinner?" Mr. Craven asked, shining the light at Clarabelle, as he lit up with a jubilant, unde-feated smile.

Clarabelle shielded her eyes. "Not in my face, Dad."

"Oh right." He turned the flashlight off and placed it on the floor. "So, like I was saying, how about a pizza?"

"Where?" Clarabelle crossed her arms in a huff and walked into what appeared to be a living room. She kicked a cloth-draped sofa, dust billowing upwards in one big puff. She coughed as it rained down around her. "We're in the boondocks."

"Oh, hush now." Mrs. Craven followed her daughter, trying to maintain her composure despite the situation. "I knew we should have stopped for dinner. And called the utility company."

Mr. Craven scowled. "It's not that bad. Besides, I noticed a small village on our way up the mountain. I bet there's pizza there."

"Fine. But I'm not getting back in the car. That ride made me sick. Too many twisty roads." Clarabelle put her arm to her forehead and dramatically fell onto the sofa.

"And coyotes," Mrs. Craven said, unbuttoning the top button of her cardigan.

Clarabelle jerked upright. She listened for a howl but the chorus that had rang upon their arrival had long been silenced. Only the incessant sound of the grandfather clock (and its strange siblings on the staircase) irritated her now. "I'll rest and you can bring home a pie. But make sure its pepperoni. And don't put any onions on it. You know how I hate onions." She sat up long enough to make a gagging gesture, then flopped back down on the couch.

In the background a funny little song echoed in the house.

"Oh, how lovely," Mrs. Craven exclaimed. "The landlord must have a left a cuckoo clock for us."

"Not one. About a dozen. Plus, a big old grandfather clock." Clarabelle sighed. Who cared about the stupid clocks anyway? Besides, it didn't sound like much of a clock. It sounded more like a bird and it was calling her by name. *"She is here! My Clarabelle dear!"*

"Let's get that pizza before it gets much later. I don't want to be up until midnight." Mr. Craven took his wife's hand, and pulling her close, grabbed her by the waist. "I wouldn't want to get lost on these back roads in the dark…you never know what kind of evil lurks in the woods." He opened his mouth wide, pretending he had fangs, and pressed his lips to Mrs. Craven's neck, who playfully slapped his cheek.

"Stop that nonsense, Victor. You'll scare her." Mrs. Craven glanced at Clarabelle who was staring at them in disgust.

"You're right. I'm terrified." Clarabelle shivered.

Mrs. Craven shook her head. "Alright, missy. That's enough."

While the house was a little dark and creepy, Clarabelle didn't want to spend another moment in the car. "Go on. Shoo. Out you go."

She got up and all but pushed her parents out the door. "I'll be fine. I'm not a baby anymore."

"Well alright," Mrs. Craven said. "We'll be back shortly." She kissed her daughter's head. "Now take care and get some rest."

With that, Clarabelle watched her parents climb back into the car, saw the headlights kick on, and waved goodbye as they coasted down the hill. She promptly closed the door, locked the handle, and flopped onto the couch.

Still feeling ill, her head aching, Clarabelle fell asleep, curled up on the dusty furniture. It felt as though only a few minutes had passed, but it was hard to tell in the dark house. The clock chimed again. It sang to her, *"Oh so lonely, my one and only."*

TOCKITY-TICK

W hat a strange little song for it to sing, Clarabelle thought. *Who's ever heard of a lonely clock?* She rolled over, finding a more comfortable position. *Forget about it, it's only a dream.*

Outside the coyotes howled, the wind wailed, and branches scraped the windows, sounding like dozens of mice scurrying across the floor. Rain trickled at first, but quickly became a violent torrent of water, pounding against the house, like an unwanted guest demanding entrance at the door. Clarabelle thought of her parents and hoped they were safe in town, warm and snug in the pizzeria waiting for the pie to crisp in a hot brick oven.

As she thought of her parents, she also longed for her friends and the big city. Clarabelle grew lonely and sad.

The clock sang, *"Why so graven Clarabelle Craven?"*

How does it know I'm sad? she thought to herself. Stupid clock. It didn't know a thing. She was just fine. She wasn't sad and she didn't miss her parents and she most certainly didn't regret her decision to stay behind in the creepy, old house.

Well, maybe a little.

Clarabelle rolled around on the couch, uncomfortable, finally relenting to the fact that she'd never settle in on the stiff old piece of furniture, especially with the clock chiming the way it was. With one last roll, she fell onto the floor in a giant *thump.*

Well, that's a fine how-do-you-do, she thought to herself.

The clock sang again, *"Why so graven Clarabelle Craven?"*

Clarabelle stood, dusted off her clothes with an annoyed little *humpf,* and marched herself straight into the foyer to confront the clock. "I am not graven. Or lonely. Or sad. I'm tired and I want to sleep—" Her chin came unhinged as she stood, not in the foyer of the great Queen Anne Victorian house but, in the middle of a busy sidewalk.

Trick-or-treaters bustled past. Jack-o'-lanterns lit the paths. A blanket of clouds hovered overhead, nearly obscuring a full moon.

"Ha-ha-happy Halloween," a woman dressed in a witch's costume cackled as she passed out candy to the children at her door.

A little girl, riding a broomstick, swept past Clarabelle nearly knocking her off her feet. "Slow down there," Clarabelle called out. "The treats aren't going anywhere." She waited a few seconds to see the child's chaperone, but no adult appeared. She glanced around, quickly realizing all of the children were unsupervised. "How strange."

Clarabelle stood in awe watching the children run from house to house, collecting their candy. She'd never seen such a sight – not even in the city. Halloween there was usually in apartment buildings or grocery stores, not on the street where lampposts cast a glow as bright as the moon.

"What are you dressed as?" A boy about Clarabelle's age walked up to her wearing a long black cape lined with red fabric that appeared as silky as her grandfather's handkerchief.

Stunned, Clarabelle glanced at her clothes, then at the ground, her eyes fixed on her black rubber galoshes. She hadn't planned on trick-or-treating this year. After all, she felt a bit old for it. She also figured she wouldn't know anyone in town or if they even would be able to follow tradition in the country. How could anyone effectively trick-or-treat when the houses were separated by hills and an over-abundance of land? Clarabelle stuck her hands in her pocket, having forgotten the candy she'd stuffed there for the car ride. She pulled out two sour lemon balls, looked at the boy and smiled.

"I'm life," Clarabelle said, dropping the candy into the boy's palm. "And I've just given you lemons."

"You're weird." He shook his head, tossed the candy into his bag, and continued walking.

Clarabelle watched as he headed down a darkened street. "Wait up!" She ran after him, feeling oddly comfortable in this new town. "Can I join you, Mr. Dracula?"

The boy stopped and turned. "It's Malcolm."

"Clarabelle Craven." She shook his hand, but a weird feeling came over her.

"You'll need one of these." He handed Clarabelle an empty bag that had a black cat with yellow eyes stitched on the front.

Clarabelle shivered as she recalled the glowing eyes in the woods around her new house, and the coyotes chorusing in song. "Thanks. You had a spare?"

"You never know when you might need a second one." Malcolm cinched his own bag closed and threw it over his shoulder. "So, you're new here."

It was definitely a statement although it really should have been a question. "Arrived a little bit ago."

"I'll say." Malcolm ran his hand across his slicked-back hair. "You'll need a better costume. Can't have you standing out like a sore thumb."

Clarabelle shrugged. "I didn't bring anything with me."

"Well, I guess this is your lucky day."

Malcolm pulled a red cape with matching horns from his bag.

"A devil costume?" Clarabelle groaned. "And you just so happened to have a spare?"

"After I hit all the houses, I change and go again. Don't you?" Malcolm shrugged. "Nevermind. Don't answer that."

"You dupe them out of their candy twice?"

"Technically yes." Malcolm lifted his eye mask and winked.

"Unbelievable." Clarabelle crossed her arms. She was disgusted and somewhat impressed. "Why on earth didn't I ever think of that?"

"Because you never had to." Malcolm turned and darted off into the darkness, leaving Clarabelle stranded in the strange village by herself.

A moment later Clarabelle heard the chime of the clock. *"Come close, come hither, Clarabelle shivers."*

DON'T GET SICK

The rhyme did, in fact, make Clarabelle shiver and she didn't like it. *I'll find that clock and I'll tell it who's boss*, she thought. "Did you hear that?" Clarabelle asked as she sprinted toward her new friend.

"Hear what?" Malcolm pulled a piece of candy from his bag and took a large bite.

Clarabelle looked back over her shoulder, sure if she spoke too loudly, it would hear her. "The clock."

Malcolm dropped his candy. "We don't talk about the clock."

"Let me get that for you." Clarabelle reached down to retrieve the piece of candy but as her fingers brushed it, she could see it wasn't candy at all. It was a large, black beetle. Clarabelle gasped and pulled back as the bug scurried away into the grass. Her gaze darted toward Malcolm who was biting the head off another beetle.

"Don't worry. They taste like candy." He shoved the rest of the insect into his mouth, a barbed leg sticking out between his lips. "Besides, you get used to it."

"What are you talking about?" Clarabelle's heart began to flutter in her chest. Something was very, very wrong and she felt the urgent need to find a way out. "That's disgusting!"

Malcolm grabbed Clarabelle's hand and yanked her from the sidewalk, so they were standing between it and the woods. "Shhhh…" he whispered. "You're going to get us caught and then…" His voice trailed off and Clarabelle was glad for it. She didn't want to hear anymore. "Just be quiet and play along."

Clarabelle stared at Malcolm wide-eyed. "Is this some sort of sick prank? I don't think it's very fun—"

Malcolm threw his hand over Clarabelle's

mouth. He put a finger to his lips and just as he did, a large shadow swept across the moon. Clarabelle started to scream, and Malcolm reminded her to be quiet to which she nodded.

As soon as the shadow disappeared, Clarabelle pulled Malcom's hand away from her mouth. "What was that?" Clarabelle tensed in anticipation of another shadow.

"The Baba Yaga," Malcolm said.

Clarabelle cleared her throat. "Baba who?"

"Baba Yaga." Malcolm shoved another beetle into his mouth. "Three sisters who control this village."

"Control it?" Clarabelle put the devil ears on her head and tied the cape around her neck. "How do they do that?"

"Every Halloween they send the beasts out to stand guard."

Clarabelle coughed. "The coyotes!"

"They're not coyotes. They're werewolves," Malcolm said as he pulled his cape tighter around him. "They report back to the Baba Yaga when they find fresh, young blood."

Suddenly the clock sang to Clarabelle again. *"Waiting close. Clarabelle knows."*

"There it is again." Clarabelle's eyes grew wide. The clock creeped her out. The chimes and chanting were eerie, and she couldn't stand it. She didn't want to be here—she had to get out. All she wanted was to be home with her parents, safe and sound. Better yet, back in the big city with her friends and the comfort of the hustle and bustle.

Malcolm shook his head. "You must ignore it."

"You hear it, too, don't you?"

Malcolm nodded, slowly.

"Tell me about the clock," Clarabelle demanded.

Malcolm pulled Clarabelle into the shadows and whispered, "It's how the Baba Yaga lure the children. Once they're trapped, they become…" The expression on his face told Clarabelle everything she needed to hear.

"Werewolves," Clarabelle gasped.

"Exactly. The Baba Yaga send out their scouts, who find the next victims. The clock lures in the children and traps them here forever."

This sounded like a bunch of hocus pocus

to Clarabelle. "But how does any of this benefit the Baba Yaga?"

"Easy. The sisters steal the children's souls." Malcolm looked around before adding, "Which gives them eternal life. The Baba Yaga grow stronger with each soul they consume. Once they're strong enough, they'll take over another town until they dominate them all." He drew another beetle from his bag and ate it.

Clarabelle snarled her lip. "Why do you eat those?"

"The Baba Yaga hate beetles. If you eat them, they can't take your soul." Malcolm handed one to Clarabelle. "Don't get sick."

"This is all so disturbing," Clarabelle said under her breath, as she held a beetle in front of her lips. "And I don't believe a single word of it." The beetle squirmed and Clarabelle squealed, dropping the insect to the ground.

Malcolm scooped it up and popped it in his mouth. "Suit yourself." He started toward a little cabin with a thatched roof.

Clarabelle stood her ground and didn't budge. "I will," she said with a huff as she crossed her arms.

"Sly like the raven, Clarabelle Craven," the clock sang to her.

Clarabelle blinked. The clock was talking again, and she was determined to find the prankster. *Why yes, I am sly,* she thought. *And I'll find you yet.*

HANDS OF TIME

Malcolm knocked on a door. "Trick-or-treat." A woman dressed as a witch stood in the warm glow of the threshold leading inside her cabin. She held a bowl shaped like a cauldron in the crook of her arm. The woman scooped out a handful of beetles which she promptly dumped into Malcolm's bag.

If Malcolm is lying about the beetles and the Baba Yaga, then he's managed to get the entire village in on it, Clarabelle thought. *So, he must be telling the truth. A prank this big would be impossible to pull off.*

"Clever girl; give it a whirl," called the clock.

Clarabelle turned around. "Who's there?"

She shook her head. *No, I must ignore the clock like Malcolm warned.* But Clarabelle's head felt suddenly cloudy, like she wasn't thinking clearly.

"Don't distrust, try us you must."

"Us? Who are you?" The chant intrigued Clarabelle and she began her search for the singing clock. She wasn't sure why she cared, but she felt as though she must find it. Maybe so she could make it shut up! Perhaps, though, it was simply curiosity. It was a good thing she wasn't a cat.

As lampposts flickered overhead, Clarabelle headed in the opposite direction as her friend. She followed a path made of bricks, the spaces filled with moss and mushrooms. At the end of the path was a ramshackle house, perched atop a trio of abnormally large and tall chicken legs. A long set of stairs was the only entrance to the front door which was propped open with a broomstick.

Clarabelle climbed the rickety steps which were ripe with mold and dust. She held her breath as each stair creaked—some happily, others sadly, and some singing a song of warning. The sound of their dying voices echoed in her head.

Creeee-aaak. Crack. Creeee-aak. Crack. *"Hands of time, hear us chime."* Tickety-tock, tockety-tick.

Clarabelle was getting close! With each clicking and ticking, the clock kept rhythm with the thud-thud-thudding of her heart. The clock seemed to whisper, *"just walk, don't mock, just walk, don't mock."*

"I'm walking and I'll find you," Clarabelle called out, her voice only trembling slightly. As Clarabelle was about to take another step, something flew in front of her eyes. She blinked, coming out of her trance-like state. A bat swooped in front of her, and Clarabelle stumbled backward. Down, down, down the stairs she fell, hitting her head with a very big, and very ugly thump.

Dazed, stars floated in her vision. When they disappeared, she sat up and rubbed the back of her head. Something in the woods grabbed her attention. Perhaps it was only more stars from the fall, but Clarabelle squinted and knew right away it was really a creature with glowing eyes. If Malcolm was telling the truth, this was not a coyote. No, it was a werewolf.

Clarabelle scrambled to her feet, backing far away from the woods and the house. A little girl wearing a blue checkered dress with a red cape brushed past Clarabelle. The girl carried a picnic basket as she headed straight for the wolf.

"Little girl," Clarabelle called. "You don't want to go there!"

The child continued skipping along, completely ignoring Clarabelle's warning.

"Stop!" Clarabelle chased after the girl who skipped faster and faster. When she finally caught up to her, deep in the woods, Clarabelle grabbed the girl's shoulder.

The girl whirled around, and Clarabelle gasped. The child had glowing yellow eyes. "Cat got your tongue?" the girl said as she dangled something from her fingertips.

Clarabelle backed away, her mouth dry, and shook her head. "No, no…never mind." As her rubber wellies crunched on a twig, something grabbed Clarabelle's shoulder. She spun around to see Malcolm. "You nearly gave me a heart attack."

"The clock's taken her," Malcolm said. He grabbed the girl's basket and dumped the contents on the ground. Chocolates and fruited candy spilled onto the grass. "Soon the Baba Yaga will claim her soul."

"But that's just candy." Clarabelle grabbed a piece, her stomach growling and reminding her that she'd never had dinner. How she longed for the pizza her parents had promised.

Malcolm tried to slap the candy from Clarabelle's hand, but she held tight. "Don't touch it," he said, his brow furrowing.

Clarabelle ignored him and unwrapped the chocolate bar. She gasped when she saw the contents inside the wrapper. "Maggots!" She threw the candy into the woods, holding back the vomit that creeped up her throat. "Disgusting!"

"I tried to warn you. All of the candy goes bad as soon as it enters the village," Malcolm said as he held out his bag of beetles. "Now eat one before the Baba Yaga come for you."

"It's too late. We're already here," three voices cackled in unison.

WATCH THEM CLIMB

"It's the Baba Yaga!" Malcolm pointed toward the sky where three witches floated on broomsticks. Backlit by the moon, Clarabelle couldn't see their faces, only the silhouettes of the trio. They wore pointed hats, the witch in the center's bent in the middle and folded over. All three wore long dresses, which billowed out in the breeze.

"What do we do now?" Clarabelle inched closer to Malcolm.

The thunder of footsteps came from behind and the two friends whirled around. Hundreds of children, all in a trance-like state, marched toward the chicken-house, their footsteps all keeping time to the chimes of the clock.

"We save the kids and defeat the Baba Yaga." Malcolm dug out a handful of beetles. "Eat these and do it quick."

Clarabelle shook her head. "I can't."

"You must. Or you'll become just like them!" Malcolm pointed at the children who now began to march up the steps of the three-legged house.

"Watch them climb, Clarabelle sublime," the clock said.

Clarabelle shook her head. "No way!" She swiped a beetle from Malcolm, closed her eyes, and popped the insect in her mouth. It crawled around on her tongue before she swallowed it whole.

Malcolm stared wide-eyed. "Next time you'll want to chew it first." He handed her another bug.

"Why is that?" Clarabelle took the insect and as she was about to pop it into her mouth, the first one flew out.

"That's why," Malcolm said with a laugh. "And now a perfectly good one has gotten away."

Clarabelle coughed. "Impossible." The second bug wiggled between her fingertips and she squinted hard as she chomped into it. "And disgusting." She frowned as she swallowed, and the beetle inched its way down her throat.

"Now hurry," Malcolm said, grabbing Clarabelle's hand and pulling her away from the witches who were ushering the children up the stairs and into the house.

Clarabelle's galoshes made a squishing sound with each step she took. "What's your plan?"

"I don't have one." Malcolm threw his bag over his shoulder and he sprinted back into the village where the streets were well-lit by lampposts.

Clarabelle raced to catch up to him. "What do you mean you don't have a plan? I thought—"

"Forget what you thought. We needed to get out of there before the Baba Yaga took us, too." Malcolm leaned against a lamppost, steadying himself as he popped another beetle into his mouth.

"But all of those kids." Clarabelle's heart lodged in her throat. "We can't just let the Baba Yaga take them."

Malcolm handed Clarabelle a beetle. "We need to build up our immunity."

Clarabelle took it and ate it but felt more disgusted than ever. "How come those children don't know the secret about the beetles? Maybe we should tell them."

"It's not like they don't know. Their bags are crawling with bugs."

"Then why aren't they eating them?" Clarabelle scratched her neck, the itchy feeling of the beetle's legs clung to her throat.

"Same reason you didn't want to. Besides, they fell victim to the clock's calls and now they're under the spell of the Baba Yaga. It's not like they'd eat the beetles willingly." Malcolm shrugged and fished around in his bag for another bug. "Last one." He held it out for Clarabelle who curled her lip as she shook her head. "Suit yourself. But you don't see me under the spell of the Baba Yaga, do you?"

Clarabelle turned and stared at her friend. He had a point. But something didn't feel quite right about all of this. Something felt a little too convenient. Malcolm was the only boy who hadn't been put under the spell. The only other kid in this crazy, weird village to even pay any attention to her. The only one eating bugs. And yet, despite it, he ran from the Baba Yaga when he was supposedly protected because of his large consumption of beetles.

"Then how come I'm not under the spell?" Clarabelle put a hand on her hip, indignant. She wasn't a fool. Even if she felt foolish for believing Malcolm all this time.

Malcolm shook his head. "You've ignored the clock, haven't you? Ignore the clock, break the spell. Eat the beetles, save your soul."

Maybe there was something to this nonsense. Maybe not. Or Maybe Malcolm was duping her. "Give it to me," Clarabelle said, grabbing for the bug. She didn't really think it would save her but if it convinced Malcolm that she was playing his game, then that's what she'd have to do. Because Clarabelle was convinced Malcolm was one of the Baba Yaga's minions.

"Too late." Malcolm ate the beetle in one swift chomp.

DING DONG

"All right, Malcolm," Clarabelle said, stepping closer and pointing her finger at his face. "I know you're helping the witches. You're like the werewolves – you're just another one of their puppets!" This wasn't a situation Clarabelle wanted any part of. She wanted out and she'd find a way. She needed to do it fast and outsmart Malcolm before he turned her over to the Baba Yaga.

Malcolm tipped his head back and laughed. "What makes you think that?"

There were too many reasons to name but Clarabelle started with the most obvious. "Just look at you! You ran away from the Baba Yaga even though you have immunity."

This made Malcolm squirm. "How many beetles had you consumed when we escaped?"

Clarabelle crossed her arms. "Two." It's not like she hadn't eaten any. Perhaps she had some immunity. She'd had a sour attitude about leaving the city and Clarabelle was willing to bet her soul wasn't desirable, with or without the beetles.

"Technically one. The first flew off. Remember?"

"Fine." Clarabelle narrowed her eyes. Malcolm was correct. Still, she'd swallowed one bug. That should account for something. "So how many do you actually have to eat?

"Thirteen."

"And how do you know this?" Clarabelle was sure Malcolm was making this up.

"Because that's precisely how long I've been stuck here. Thirteen years has given me plenty of time to make mistakes. But it's also given me time to learn the ropes. And to discover that the clock stops chiming at twelve. Thirteen is the magic number. Make it to that and you'll live to see another Halloween."

"But you can't be any older than eleven." Clarabelle felt impatient as she shifted from foot to foot, her galoshes making that weird squishing sound like she'd stepped in something gross. There were children to save but she had to get to the bottom of this before she could do anything. When the boy didn't respond, Clarabelle added, "You've been here that long?"

Malcolm nodded. "Time is different in the village."

Things were about as strange as they could get but Clarabelle had an idea. Really it was a simple solution and she couldn't understand why Malcolm hadn't thought of it himself. "Do you think we can get each of the children to eat thirteen beetles?" She ran up to the cabin with the thatched roof and rang the doorbell. Ding dong. "I'll start here and fill my bag." She waited a moment before resorting to knocking on the door. No one answered.

"Don't waste your time." Malcolm chuckled at his pun. "Everyone locks up precisely at nine."

This was the most ridiculous thing Clarabelle had ever heard. There were witches known to the village as the Baba Yaga who stole the souls of children on Halloween, using a clock to lure them in but only after werewolves scouted them out, and they closed up shop with the most valuable resource by nine o'clock. Who were these crazy people? "Then how will I be protected if I'm going to save the children?"

"We'll have to scavenge for them." Malcolm knelt down and parted a patch of grass. He snatched a bug and handed it to Clarabelle. "There's only three hours remaining. Once the clock strikes twelve, those children will belong to the Baba Yagas forever. We'll need to hurry."

Clarabelle and Malcolm worked quickly, plucking beetles from the grass, the sidewalks, and under leaves, until they'd found a full dozen.

"Here goes nothing," Clarabelle said as she ate the bugs one by one. When she finished, she looked at Malcolm, both horrified and disgusted. "I can't believe I did that. Twelve of them! Blech!"

"Thirteen. A baker's dozen." Malcolm removed his mask and it fell to the ground. "You'll be safe now." He smiled at Clarabelle who, for the first time, had a good long look at this strange bug-eating boy. He had freckles which Clarabelle hadn't noticed while he wore his mask. Malcolm also had green eyes, something she felt was quite unique. She'd seen hazel, of course, like her own, but never green.

She smiled back. "Then what are we waiting for? Let's go!" Clarabelle started to run off toward the Baba Yaga's strange looking chicken-legged house, deep in the woods.

"Not so fast," Malcolm called, running up to her. "We really do need a plan."

"We feed them bugs," Clarabelle said. "Don't they have them in their bags?"

"Even if we could convince them to eat thirteen beetles, it would take forever and there's just not enough time."

Clarabelle paced the sidewalk. "Then what do you suggest we do?"

"I don't know," Malcolm said with a shrug.

"You mean to tell me you've been here thirteen years and you've never figured out a way to save the children?"

"Well you try and escape from three hags under pressure. You're lucky I discovered the bug thing. That's kept me safe for the last two years."

Clarabelle suddenly stopped in her tracks.

"But have you figured out a way to escape that?" She pointed at a set of yellow eyes peering out from behind a tree. "Or how about that one?" Another set of eyes glowed in the grass. Four more sets popped up and Clarabelle backed into Malcolm, the two friends bracing against each other. They were surrounded by a pack of very large, very fierce werewolves.

IT SNEAKS ALONG

"Well? I'm waiting." Clarabelle elbowed Malcolm in the back.

"That's easy," he said. "Like this." Malcom made a chiming noise that sounded eerily similar to the clock. The werewolves perked their ears. Then they lifted their muzzles into the air and howled.

"I think it's working," Clarabelle said. She clucked her tongue, making a ticking sound. The wolves turned their heads and took off in a sprint toward the house of the witch sisters.

The two friends high-fived each other.

"We did it!" Malcolm said as he leapt into the air.

Clarabelle raised an eyebrow. "You had no idea that would work, did you?"

"None at all." Malcolm smirked. "Now, let's go! We've got kids to save."

"But we just sent the werewolves toward the Baba Yaga house. We can't go that way, or we're done for. Plus, we need a plan. Remember?"

Malcolm pushed up the sleeves of his sweatshirt. "Good point."

Clarabelle felt confident there was a way to save the children without sacrificing themselves to the werewolves. They were both protected from the witches, all thanks to those nasty beetles. Maybe if they found a way to armor themselves from the animals, then they could go straight into the den. Otherwise, they'd need to approach this in another fashion. "Do you have any ideas?"

"Maybe we could sneak up behind the house? The werewolves won't see us there and the Baba Yaga will be too busy with their soul-sucking to notice us." Malcolm didn't look overly confident with his proposal and he cleared his throat, his cheeks flushing.

"Wouldn't work." Clarabelle shook her

head. "We'd still need to climb the stairs to get into the Baba Yaga house. That's where the clock is."

Malcolm's eyes widened. "That's it!"

"What is?" Clarabelle furrowed her brow.

"We have to destroy the clock!" Malcolm shook Clarabelle's shoulder. "It's genius!"

Clarabelle was sure she'd never understand this strange bug-eating boy. "Impossible. We have to enter the house to get to the clock. We'd never go unnoticed unless we tried to blend in."

Malcolm shook his head. "The clock is just a decoy. The heart of it is deep in the forest. When I first arrived thirteen years ago and saw what the Baba Yagas were doing, I ran to the hills and hid out in the caves. As I had made my way through the woods, I saw the clock's heart. Of course, I didn't know what it was at that time but now I'm convinced it's what keeps the clock living and breathing."

"You mean to tell me the clock is alive?"

"In a sense it is. Everything has something that keeps it going. A heart, a soul, a brain. Energy, matter."

"Or a curse." Clarabelle sighed. "So, we go

to the forest, find the heart of the clock, kill it, and everyone is free. Sounds simple enough."

Malcolm sat on the sidewalk and put his head between his knees. "Nothing is that easy here. There's got to be something I'm missing."

Clarabelle agreed. Usually something that vital had protection. Whether it be a giant troll that stood guard or a magic spell that encased it, there's no way it would be as easy as just destroying the clock's heart. Someone would have done that long ago if it was. "There's no other option, though, is there? Maybe we should try it anyway."

"It's worth a shot." Malcolm leapt to his feet and grabbed Clarabelle's hand. "It's this way!" He darted off between two houses, dragging Clarabelle with him before she let go and kept pace at his side.

The deeper they went into the forest, the darker it got. The leafless trees created a thick canopy of branches which obscured the moon.

"I feel like we might be lost," Clarabelle said, glancing around her. She'd never seen a forest like this before. Technically, she hadn't seen a forest ever, so she wasn't sure if her surroundings were normal or not. "Are you sure we're going the right way?"

"I'm positive," Malcolm said as leaves and twigs crunched beneath his sneakers.

"But you've only ever seen it once. How can you know?"

Malcolm took a deep breath. "Trust me. You don't forget something like this."

"It's that bad?" Clarabelle paused, her breath hitching in her throat.

Malcolm stopped at the base of a tree and turned around, watching Clarabelle who stared up into the branches arching across the trail. "We don't have to do this. Children come every year, the Baba Yaga steal their souls, and then all is quiet until the following Halloween. It's not like I haven't seen it over and over again. It sneaks along."

"We can't let them die." Clarabelle turned away, not wanting Malcolm to read the expression on her face. He might learn she missed her family. She also didn't want to be stuck in this wicked village for thirteen years like him. For all she knew, she could be stuck forever.

"Then it's this way." Malcolm lurched

forward and Clarabelle followed close at his side.

They pressed forward through the darkness of night, past gangly-looking trees, waist-tall bushes, and damp leaves which smelled of earth. The closer they were to finding the clock's heart, the more Clarabelle felt unease and the more she believed the clock was singing to her. She knew she couldn't tell Malcolm, or he'd insist they stop. That wasn't a chance Clarabelle could take.

"Don't be afraid, we'll make a trade," the clock sang.

Clarabelle shook her head and thought, *be quiet! This isn't real.*

"I'll take the boy and you'll be free, that's the promise of the three."

"I can't hear you!" Clarabelle shouted.

Malcolm stopped suddenly and stood frozen like a statue.

"What's the matter?" Clarabelle tapped his shoulder.

Malcolm turned around. His eyes were yellow.

DONGITY-DING

"Malcolm!" Clarabelle shook him as she screamed. "Wake up! Don't listen to it!"

The boy blinked and gazed at Clarabelle confused.

"The clock almost took you," Clarabelle said.

Malcolm rubbed his head. "It promised that I'd be free if I turned you over."

"Are you sure?" Clarabelle gasped. "Because it told me the same thing about you."

"It's not to be trusted." Malcolm grabbed his stomach and hunched over.

Clarabelle rushed to his side. "What's wrong?"

"Think I ate too many beetles. I'll be fine. Just give me a second."

There wasn't time to spare and they both knew it. "I'll go on without you. I think I can find it from here." Clarabelle wasn't sure she could, but she knew she had to try. If she listened to the clock's calls and objected along the way, she may just be able to stay safe. She'd find the clock's heart, destroy it, and set them all free. Then she could go home. Even if it wasn't in the big city with her friends.

Malcolm rolled on the ground and groaned. "Are you sure?"

"I've got this." Clarabelle pushed up her sleeves and marched toward the clock's call. With each taunt, Clarabelle resisted, only giving enough to bait the clock into revealing it's hiding spot. She turned between two tall Oak trees, their leafless branches looking like skeletons.

"Closer Clarabelle, you're in my spell," the clock sang with a dongity-ding.

"Yes, I am, old clock. I'm coming." Clarabelle's head hurt from resisting, but she had to press forward. Only she could save the children from the Baba Yaga. She traced her hand along the rocky surface of the mountainside, as she walked uphill. Then she saw the glow. A slow burn at first but then a flash of color. She knew what it was even before she reached it. Clarabelle rushed up and there, in a crevice of the rocky mountainside, was the clock's heart.

To Clarabelle's surprise, it wasn't actually a heart, as she had expected. It wasn't really a clock either. And yet it was. "What even are you?" Clarabelle asked as she stared at the hideous heart of the clock.

The clock's heart was actually a glowing head of an old, old man. It was encased in glass that somewhat resembled the face of a clock. Crooked, wrinkly fingers pointed at the minutes while a fat, warty nose popped out on a spring when the hour chimed. It all glowed an eerie shade of blue.

The heart gasped when it saw Clarabelle. "Go away!" It yelled.

Clarabelle refused to budge and the two stared at each other for a long while.

"What an awful, wretched thing!" Clarabelle's lip snarled in disgust as she reached into the crevice. She hardly wanted to touch it, but she had no choice. It must be destroyed. As soon as she wrapped her hands around the clock's heart, she felt funny. Like she'd faded away…disappeared.

"Drop it," Malcolm screamed.

Clarabelle turned and looked at him. She tried to speak but couldn't. There seemed to be a strange distance to everything, like she was on the wrong side of the glass at the zoo.

Malcolm swatted the clock's heart from Clarabelle's hands, and it fell to the ground, cracking the glass encasing the head.

Clarabelle blinked. "What's wrong with you? I could have saved them."

"You almost destroyed *yourself*," Malcolm said. "You were fading. I should have known. Destroy the heart, ruin us all. It's the witches we need to go after. We break the spell and set us all free." He rolled the clock's heart with his foot, turning it upright. Through the large crack, the face scowled at him. It wasn't broken, just damaged. He scooped it up with his trick-or-treat bag, tucked it inside, and threw it over his shoulder.

"But that's impossible. You said so yourself."

"No." Malcolm shook his head. "I said it was impossible to feed all of the children thirteen beetles. I thought it would be easier to destroy the heart then it would be to defeat the witches. I had no idea it could backfire."

"It's too late now. We'll never break the curse and I'll be stuck here forever." Clarabelle felt tears forming in her eyes and she held her breath to make them stop. She wasn't a baby and now wasn't the time to start behaving like one, either.

"Don't say that. We can't give up." Malcolm squeezed Clarabelle's shoulder. "You're the first person I've found who was able to help me. It's not like it's been a picnic the last thirteen years."

Clarabelle looked at her new friend. She hadn't considered him in any of this. She'd thought of the children and of herself, but not him. "Do you think we can do it in time?"

Malcolm straightened his collar, fastened his cape tighter, and stood up straighter. "We have to try."

"Then let's do this thing!" Clarabelle started running through the forest with Malcolm close behind. "We've got witches to burn."

IT DOESN'T RING

C larabelle and Malcolm reached the chicken-house and hid behind a tree as they watched the children march inside. The three witches, which Clarabelle could now see clearly, were just as hideous as she had imagined. Grayish skin, pointed noses, and stringy black hair. The tallest one with the bent hat seemed to be the leader as the other two obeyed her commands.

"Are you sure this will work?" Clarabelle asked Malcolm as they stayed tucked behind the tree. Hundreds of children, all dressed in their Halloween costumes, swarmed the Baba Yaga house. The children were nothing more than brainless zombies. The poor things had no idea of the fate that awaited them.

Malcolm cleared his throat. "No, not really. But I'm willing to try."

"Then let's go."

"Put these on," Malcolm said, handing Clarabelle a pair of dark sunglasses. "The Baba Yaga won't be able to see our eyes."

"And then they won't know we're not under the spell."

Malcolm stood. "Exactly!"

The two friends pushed their way through the hoard of children. When they reached the stairs of the Baba Yaga chicken-legged house, they paused.

"Don't forget what we talked about," Malcolm said.

Clarabelle lowered her glasses and winked. "You can count on me."

Malcolm and Clarabelle clasped each other's hands and made their way toward the witches. Two were each stirring their own large black cauldrons on opposite sides of the kitchen. Clarabelle squeezed Malcom's hand. He then surrendered his trick-or-treat bag before she snuck down a dark corridor.

The small, run-down house suddenly felt much larger than it looked on the outside. Clarabelle paused, swallowing her fear and listened for the clock. Surely it would call to her now. As she swept the room, a reflection bounced off a window and Clarabelle's heart leapt in her chest.

"Time's a fleeting, your heart's beating."

Hearing its taunt, Clarabelle walked cautiously into the dark room. There were hundreds of clocks on the wall. Cuckoo clocks of all shapes and sizes, with strange carvings. Instead of a bird that popped out, some had bats while others had spiders and skulls. Clarabelle shivered. She turned slowly, studying each one. She had to find it and fast. One clock was missing a face. "I've found it!" she whispered.

Malcolm rushed into the room. "Good job. You know what you need to do."

The tall, coffin-shaped clock made Clarabelle's skin crawl, but she reached out to touch its curved lines and heard the clock whisper once more.

"The hour is near, Clarabelle dear." The clock's

song deepened, the words stretching out in slow-motion.

Clarabelle gasped. The ticking of the clock grew louder and louder and it seemed as if it would drive Clarabelle mad. A chill ran across her skin. She felt cold and her hands were clammy as she fumbled around in the bag.

The clock sang again. *"Mine, all mine, Clarabelle divine."*

No, I'm not yours, she thought, but her tongue was too twisted to call out.

"Hurry, Clarabelle," Malcolm said, urging her to complete the work.

Clarabelle gripped the clock's heart in her hands. The world around her swirled, her head felt dizzy, her brain in a fog. She knew she must run, escape from this house, get away from the clock, but her body wouldn't cooperate. Clarabelle was trapped.

Then the clock sang once more, *"Clarabelle Craven why so graven?"*

Malcolm stepped closer. "Go on, Clarabelle! You can do it."

Grumbling and groaning, the mumbling voices of the witches came down the hall.

"Claaa-raaa-belle, where are you?" Three sets of footsteps accompanied the Baba Yaga calls.

"Don't tell us," one of the witches laughed. "I *like* games."

"Hide and seek," another witch said. "It's my favorite."

"Shut up, you two," the witch-in-charge shouted. "We'll find her, take her soul, and live forever." Her cackle was so loud it shattered the glass of a clock.

Clarabelle blinked, fear flooding through her body. Her head felt funny. But she saw Malcolm, and she remembered she was supposed to do something. But she couldn't recall what. It all seemed like a distant memory.

Malcolm suddenly shoved into her. "Hurry, the witches are coming!"

Her hands trembled, shaking the clock's heart. "Witches!" Clarabelle gasped as it all came flooding back. She shoved the heart inside the body of the coffin.

The clock made horrible noises, ticking, tocking, dinging, donging.

Then it stopped.

"It doesn't ring," Malcolm said.

The witches snaked their way into the room. When they saw the children, they squealed. "Dinnertime!"

"Not anymore," Malcolm pointed to the clock and the witches shrieked.

"Look what you've done!" the witch with the bent hat screamed. "You'll pay for this!" She began to melt away into the floor. The sisters turned into puffs of smoke and disappeared.

Clarabelle stood there, unable to move as she was completely frozen in place. Her eyes flickered as the clock chimed, twelve times. "Did it work? Did we break the spell?" Clarabelle shuddered, and fell to the ground. Then the world went black.

Hours later, Clarabelle sat up, and rubbed her eyes.

"Did you have a good nap?" Mrs. Craven asked as the room glowed softly with candle light. "You've been asleep for hours."

"Turned out the landlord didn't turn off the electricity. Just had to find the circuit breaker." Mr. Craven flipped a switch and the room lit up.

"Even the television works," Mrs. Craven said with a smile. "I can put on something spooky if you want. I know how you have your Halloween movie traditions."

Clarabelle shook her head.

Mr. Craven handed Clarabelle a paper plate with a slice of pepperoni pizza. "What's the matter? Cat got your tongue?"

"No...no...I'm fine," Clarabelle said, shaking her head. This was too unreal. Clarabelle was so relieved to know that the witches, the clock, the werewolves...all of it...was just the most terrifying nightmare of all time. Her breath caught in her throat. "Malcolm," she whispered. He felt like a real friend and she missed him.

"Everything all right?" Mrs. Craven asked.

Clarabelle leapt off the couch and hugged her parents. "Everything is fine. It's wonderful. It couldn't be better."

Mrs. Craven smiled at her, and said, "Clarabelle Craven, your safe haven."

Clarabelle took a large bite of the pizza. "It's still warm." She smiled. When she'd devoured the entire slice, she went to the table for another. Thirteen beetles skittered away. Clarabelle blinked. "Impossible."

Then, from the foyer, came the loud gongs of the grandfather clock as it chimed the nine o'clock hour.

A NOTE FROM THE AUTHOR

I first wrote this as a short story back in 2012. At the time it was a mere 2,500 words (about five pages long). The story was then published online as The Tale of Annabelle Craven. I'd nearly forgotten about the story until recently when I decided to revive it. Finding it was another problem! After relentless searches, I finally located the story. With some world building, a slight change of name for my female lead, and a lot of work, the story lives again!

There's always a range of emotions when releasing a new book. Aside from the excitement and anticipation there's always fear and worry. I hope that if you enjoyed this book, you'll leave a review. Reviews help authors find new readers, and leads readers to great new stories.

Thanks for reading my work! As always, many, many thanks for your support!

— AMIE BORST

ABOUT THE AUTHOR

Amie Borst believes in unicorns, loves glitter, and keeps a stash of chocolate hidden away from her chocolate-stealing family. She is the author of several books for children including the Scarily Ever Laughter series (Cinderskella, Little Dead Riding Hood, Snow Fright), the Unicorn Tales series, and the Doomy Prepper series. She's a founding member of From the Mixed-Up Files of Middle-Grade Authors where she contributed for nearly a decade. Please visit her website for more information about school visits and speaking engagements. While you're there, be sure to sign up for her newsletter so you can receive updates on new books, sales, and promotions.

Website: www.amieborst.com

ALSO BY AMIE BORST

Scarily Ever Laughter series:

1 - Cinderskella

2 - Little Dead Riding Hood

3 - Snow Fright

Doomy Prepper series:

1 -Doomy Prepper's Complete Guide: How to Survive Fifth Grade and the Apocalypse

Unicorn Tales series:

1 - Callie's Magical Flight

2 - Maeve's New Friend

Made in the USA
Columbia, SC
07 December 2019

84517256R00050